The Magic of

PAULA
ABDUL

FROM STRAIGHT UP
TO *SPELLBOUND!*

D1315198

The Magic of

PAULA ABDUL

FROM STRAIGHT UP TO *SPELLBOUND!*

A Biography by Devra Newberger

SCHOLASTIC INC.
New York Toronto London Auckland Sydney

For Adam: Hey "U" — I Do!

Photo Credits

Cover photos: © Neal Preston/Outline Press.

Inside cover photos: Courtesy Virgin Records/Alberto Tolot.

Inside photo spread: Page 1: Courtesy Virgin Records/Glen Erler. Page 2: © Timothy White/Onyx (top); © Photography Inc. (bottom). Page 3: © Diana Lyn 1991/Shooting Star (top); courtesy Virgin Records (bottom). Page 4: © Charles William Bush/Shooting Star. All rights reserved. Page 5: © Rob Brown/Onyx (both). Page 6: Courtesy Virgin Records. Page 7: © Steve Granitz/Retina Ltd. (both). Page 8: Courtesy Virgin Records/Alberto Tolot (top left and right); © Timothy White/Onyx (center).

ISBN 0-590-45443-9

12 11 10 9 8 7 6 5 4 3 2   1 2 3 4 5 6/9

Printed in the U.S.A.   01

First Scholastic printing, October 1991

Contents

The Magic of
PAULA ABDUL

FROM STRAIGHT UP
TO *SPELLBOUND!*

Introduction:
Rush, Rush to the Top!

Most mornings, Paula Abdul's routine seems, for the most part, normal: She wakes up, brushes her teeth, showers, and gets dressed.

But on other mornings, this 28-year-old dynamic dancing sensation has moments that are anything *but* normal. Admittedly, Paula claims to have had some of her most inspirational ideas while brushing her teeth! Sometimes, she says, she'll get busy right there at that sink, working out some funky, new dance steps while still in her pj's, toothbrush in hand!

There's no denying it: Paula Abdul leads one of the busiest lives in show business. Why else would she feel compelled to bust a move at 5 A.M. in the bathroom? From the moment she wakes, till the second her

1

pretty head hits the pillow at night, this gal is busy, busy, busy! With more projects in the works than there are hyphens in her title, this singer-dancer-choreographer-director-producer's dance card is completely booked solid . . . well into 1994!

Maybe that's why Paula has kept us waiting so long for a follow-up album to her smash LP, *Forever Your Girl*. With such a truly terrific debut explosion, was it any wonder the world begged for more? But then, as it is pretty obvious by now . . . her newest album, *Spellbound*, was well worth the wait!

Few artists have had such a successful debut album as Paula. Literally, Paula rode the wave of success from *Forever Your Girl* for nearly two and a half years! With one solid gold hit after another, the album just busted up the charts, selling over *ten million* copies worldwide. And even when one of her slammin' dance tracks slipped from its Number One chart position, there was always another awesome Paula tune close behind to fill the void. One disc jockey noted that Paula had managed to keep a succession of singles in the Top 40 for a whopping 66 straight weeks!

Spawning four Number One singles,

Forever Your Girl spent over 100 weeks on the *Billboard* charts, and rested comfortably in the Number One album spot for ten of those weeks, helping to earn this tornado-in-toe-shoes a name for herself in the music biz — not to mention a batch of prestigious awards. And now, with *Spellbound* casting its magic upon the world, and as Paula kicks off her very first world-tour spectacular, all we can do is wait once again — to see if her hit-making history repeats itself!

1.
Paula's First Steps

Ten years ago, if you had told Paula's mom, Lorraine Abdul, that her daughter would grow up to become one of the most famous dancer-choreographers in the world, she would have laughed!

"Even though she'd outdance everyone," says Lorraine, "Paula never fit anyone's idea of a tall, leggy dancer." She does admit, though, that she never, ever doubted her sweet daughter would become something special. "Even as a baby," she remembers, "people would stop me to look at her. The charm was there; everyone wanted to be around her."

"Being short," says Paula, "and wanting to be a dancer is like, unheard of. Everyone always said, 'You're never gonna make it in the dance world.' But my mother taught me early on that the key is never giving up. And I didn't! I faced a lot of rejection and it was always hard, but when everyone said I wouldn't make it, I said, 'Yes I am! I'm going to make it.' "

She remembers the hardest part of her struggle to make it as a dancer: the auditions. It wasn't so easy going into an audition, when even some of her dance instructors had told her that casting agents would never give her a chance, and never see beyond her size and shape.

"The humiliation of lining up in a line," Paula recalls, "knowing that I *can* dance and that I *can* do that choreography, and wanting just a chance to do it. But being cut because of my height or because of the way that I look — even before I could give it a shot and show them I could dance — it was rejection over and over again."

Born on June 19, 1963, Paula was the second daughter for Harry and Lorraine Abdul. The Abduls — Harry, Lorraine, Paula, and Paula's older sister, Wendy, lived in a nice, suburban section of North Hollywood, California, in the San Fernando Valley. Harry, a livestock trader, and Lorraine, a movie studio director's assistant, tried their best to provide a loving, caring environment for their two girls.

Unfortunately, as it happens to many families, Paula's mom and dad split up when Paula was seven. Both Paula and Wendy stayed with their mother. "I saw my dad on weekends," Paula explains, "but I missed him a lot. Especially during the first few weeks."

Growing up, Paula recalls the exact moment she decided that leading the glamorous life of a Hollywood musical dancer was for her. "I was the kid that didn't really get into playing with Barbie dolls and stuffed animals," she says. "I was, at a very early age, really into watching musicals!"

As four-year-old Paula sat on the living room couch in between her parents, she became mesmerized watching actor Gene Kelly dance up a storm in the movie *Singin' in the Rain*. "That was it for me," Paula said, "watching Gene Kelly. At that moment, I knew I wanted to be an entertainer like him. He seemed to be having so much fun. I'd actually dream about being in scenes, singing and dancing with [him]!"

But it was Wendy who donned the first pair of dance shoes in the family. When her sister went to her lessons each week, seven-year-old Paula tagged along. "Even as a little one," Lorraine recalls, "she would sit and watch her sister's dance group. Then she'd come home and recreate everything she saw. Show her once, and she had it."

Wendy agrees with her mother. "Within a few months," Wendy says, "Paula outshone everyone." Dance lessons for Paula didn't formally begin until one year later.

Paula's mom remembers how her daughter begged and begged and begged for dance lessons. Once, Paula was supposed to go to her friend's house after school to play. But her friend's mother had forgotten that her daughter had a dance lesson that day. She called Lorraine on the phone and asked if Paula could go along with them. Lorraine agreed.

"I picked them up [from the lesson]," Lorraine remembers, "and all I heard on the way home was, 'I have to take dancing! I have to take dancing!'"

Of course, at this point, Paula's parents knew their daughter had an obsession with the art. How could they say no? They decided that Paula was now old enough to take formal lessons, and agreed to let her take a few classes. And before you could say "arabesque," Paula was enrolled in ballet, tap, and modern dance classes! "She would never miss a class," says her mother. "It could be pouring, the brakes on my car shot, and Paula was in the car in tears, afraid she was going to be late!" Not long after, Paula also signed up for jazz and classical dance. One of her dance teachers from back then, Dean Barlow, still works with Paula today. He's helped her with quite a few projects, as an advisor.

One of Paula's fondest childhood memories happened when she was around eight years old. She entered a tap-dancing contest, singing and tapping her heart out to "Yankee Doodle Dandy." Obviously, she must have had talent back then, too, because she took first place!

In elementary school, all of Paula's teachers recognized her dance talents and her knack for choreography. Whenever the school held plays and other performances, they called on Paula to help with the dance direction. "I was into choreography before I even knew what it was," she laughs. She remembers appearing in the school productions of *Oklahoma!*, *West Side Story*, and *Seven Brides for Seven Brothers*.

Outside of school, Paula was very involved in the community theater, which, she says, included lots of dancing, too. In the summers, she toured the country, acting in theater productions. At age ten, she was such a good dancer in her jazz and tap classes that she won a scholarship to study under Joe Tramie and the prestigious Bella Lewitzky Company.

High school proved to be an exciting time for this outgoing, super-popular girl. She attended Van Nuys High School — the same school, Paula likes to point out, that Marilyn Monroe and Robert Redford went to! Paula spent her high school years involved in just about everything. In addition to making the cheerleading team, she was elected head cheerleader! "She used to have the girls come over in the backyard and work, work, work," says her mom. "Everything always had to look great."

She was also a member of the speech club, science club, and debate team, and still managed to keep up a terrific grade point average. And if this musical maven didn't already have enough extracurricular activities to handle, she also found time to play flute in the school orchestra! "I was the junior class president, head cheerleader, homecoming princess, and May queen," the pop star remembers. "All that disgusting stuff . . . but I loved it!" In her senior year, this popular miss was also elected senior-class president and voted "Most Likely to Succeed."

Last year, Paula got an invitation to her ten-year high school reunion. Of course everyone in the Van Nuys High School Class of '80 figured this mega-star would be a no-show . . . but Paula fooled them all. "I was vacillating back and forth," she says. "Should I go? Shouldn't I go? In the end, I went. And it was both funny and strange. I wanted to go to my reunion because I wanted to see my friends that I had lost touch with. My high school years were very important to me. [At the reunion] people came up to me and said, 'I'm so glad you haven't changed.'" The evening turned out to be a warm, emotional night for Paula — a time to reminisce with her high school pals way into the wee hours!

2.
From Valley Girl
to Laker Girl

By the end of Paula's senior year in high school, this 5′2″ cutie was graduating with an impressive 3.85 grade point average. But then she was faced with that all-important, inevitable question: What next?

Paula had been a good enough student in high school to earn a scholarship to college.

"I always knew that I wanted to be in show business," Paula explains, "but I wanted to have something to fall back on." So she enrolled at California State in Northridge and set out to major in TV and radio broadcasting. "I thought I'd go into broadcasting," she said, "and become the next Jayne Kennedy."

She still remembers how determined she was to make it as a broadcaster, devoting long hours and hard work to her courses. But as things sometimes happen, she became sidetracked — by a diversion that would eventually lead her down the road to fame and fortune!

During her freshman year at Cal State, a good friend of Paula's heard of auditions that were being held for the Los Angeles Lakers basketball team cheerleaders — the Laker Girls. On a whim, Paula decided to try out.

When she arrived at the auditions, Paula was downright nervous. Because of her height, she had never imagined that she could become a professional dancer, so when she took a look at the other girls who had come to try out, her confidence went right out the door. (And *she* almost did, too!) There were 500 other girls there, and most of them, Paula says, were tall, beautiful, and older. At first, Paula was so intimidated that she figured she would just sit by and watch the other girls audition.

After a while of sitting on the sidelines, Paula thought to herself, "Wait a minute . . . I can do that . . . and better!" So she took her rightful position on the dance floor and prepared to blow the judges away! And despite the fact that there were 500 tall, beautiful, older gals trying out that day, it was Paula who caused quite a commotion!

"She was such a great dancer," remembers Lon Rosen, the former Lakers publicist (now the manager for awesome Lakers guard Magic Johnson), who hired Paula. "She was really slick." And by the end of the day, Paula and eleven other girls had made the squad! She was an honest-to-goodness Laker Girl, and was handed a uniform to prove it.

It wasn't long before the other Laker Girls and the Lakers administration realized just how incredibly talented Paula was. "Within three weeks," remembers Lon Rosen, "she became the choreographer! I think we even gave her a raise from $500 to $550 a month." Paula was ecstatic!

"Choreographing for the Laker Girls gave me the perfect outlet to experiment with all the ideas I had," she says. "I was this cheerleader who kind of broke the rules. I wanted to get rid of the pom-pom thing, focus more on dance. This stereotypical cheerleading thing always bothered me a lot — teased-up hair and sexy bodies. It didn't matter how well you danced, nothing mattered as long as you were a beautiful bombshell. I never was that, and I was always the underdog." Not anymore! With her new position as choreographer, she felt as if she were on top of the world.

Paula's choreography for the squad was sensational. She slowly moved away from those typical pom-pom moves, creating more hard-edged, jazzy, street-inspired steps. Although she was carrying a heavy course load at school, Paula completely dove headfirst into her work with the Laker Girls. The best part was, it was she who was in charge, calling all the shots! "I was able to create whatever I wanted at the Laker games," she says. And with Paula at the helm, halftime at the Forum took on a whole new look.

As choreographer, she had the opportunity to become accustomed to working behind the camera — something she definitely makes good use of today. "Anytime a routine was being shown," she says, "I was able to work with the camera crews and tell them to get a wide-angle shot of this or that. I would have the girls work in different formations, just so the crew would get used to it and block it."

Six months after joining the Laker Girls, Paula was faced with a very tough decision.

Balancing both school and work had become way too exhausting — physically and emotionally. It was at that point that she chose to drop out of college in order to dance and choreograph full time. Needless to say, her parents weren't thrilled with their daughter's decision. But they supported Paula nonetheless.

Looking back on her days with the Laker Girls, Paula says that some of her sassiest dance steps were created during the three years she choreographed for them. She even admits that she sometimes borrows her old Laker Girls stuff for her new routines! "I'll watch old footage," she says, "and I'll see something and say, 'That's pretty cool. I can update that a bit and make it even better.'" One routine, however, she vowed she would never repeat was also one of her most embarrassing moments, ever! "We were all dressed in funny fat-men outfits," she remembers, "but when we ran out onto the court, one girl bumped into Magic [Johnson], and a bunch of us fell over like dominoes! I laughed so hard . . . and I have the weakest bladder! It was soooo embarrassing!"

These days, when Paula returns to the

Los Angeles Forum to do a concert, it's a very emotional experience for the singer. "I remember all those nights when I'd arrive at the Forum, and the other girls would be coming from school or work, and we'd go out onto the floor and knock all the weird tunes out. Then we'd have dinner together at the cafeteria.

"Once," she continues, "on a night of my concert [at the Forum], I was walking through the tunnel and it was freezing. I [had to keep reminding myself] that I wasn't going out there to perform in my uniform, I was going out to go up on the stage as the *star*. It was the most amazing feeling."

Lately, though, Paula wishes she had more time to attend even one Lakers basketball game — she misses it so much. "I've hardly been able to go to any games," she says, "but they're really good to me at the Forum." So good, in fact, that there is talk of retiring Paula's uniform and hanging it from the rafters next to basketball heroes Wilt Chamberlain's and Kareem Abdul-Jabbar's!

The Forum holds a very special place in Paula's heart. For it was there that her on-court antics caught the attention of some very important people. It was there, one night at a Lakers game, that Paula Abdul's life completely changed. In one night, all her hard work and dedication began to pay off — and pay off big!

3.
Breakin' into the Biz!

Lakers basketball games are quite the spectacle in Los Angeles. Most L.A. natives are die-hard fans who never, *ever* miss a game. One such fan is actor Jack Nicholson! Paula remembers how the actor had season tickets right on the floor, but that he usually brought a pair of binoculars with him to get a closer look at the Laker Girls!

Other true-blue, purple-and-gold fans include the Jackson brothers Michael, Marlon, and Jackie. They held season tickets, too, and over time had become big fans of Paula! They were so wildly impressed with her innovative, fresh dance style that one night they asked to meet the girl behind the Laker Girls' funky steps.

Paula did meet the Jackson brothers that

evening, but an introduction wasn't all that took place. It just so happened that the Jacksons were looking for a choreographer to work out the moves for their first music video from their album *Victory*. Jackie couldn't believe his luck when Paula agreed to choreograph their "Torture" video. And Paula couldn't believe her luck — a chance to work with the most famous musical family in the world!

"They gave a kid an opportunity," Paula says of the Jacksons, "and it was an incredible experience for me." Days later, Paula was on a plane to New York to choreograph their "Torture" video. "I was a nervous wreck!" she confesses. "I wanted to pretend that I knew everything I was doing . . . but I didn't know *anything* I was doing! But the Jackson brothers were great. They knew that I was a Laker Girl and that this was my first big break. And they gave it to me! They were very supportive.

"Choreography kind of fell into my lap," she continues. "I didn't know it would become a career for me to make money. It was something I did just for fun."

Working with the Jackson brothers was just the beginning. It wasn't long before their younger sister, Janet, who was trying to break into the music business on her own, was looking for someone to help her with her dancing. No sooner had Paula returned from New York, than she was contacted by a man named John McClain. "He said to me, 'I love what you do with the Laker Girls,' " Paula recalls. " 'We have an artist who has a couple of albums . . . her name is Janet Jackson.' I just laughed and thought, 'Yes, I think I know her brothers!' "

It just so happened that Marlon, Jackie, and the other Jackson brothers simply raved about Paula, and recommended the spirited dancer-choreographer to their sister. Janet had listened to her brothers rave about Paula's unusual, hip street style, and was excited to work with her. Of course, Paula was even more excited . . . she had her next job!

Working with Janet became the turning point in Paula's own career. "When I first started working with Janet," Paula says, "a whole new style was brought out. It was a combination of what I was doing with the Laker Girls. I was mixing technical training with street movement. Everyone thought I was crazy, but once Janet's videos were seen, that's when everything hit.

"With Janet's videos," she continues, "I really got to see the influence choreography has on kids and adults. Going to clubs and seeing people emulate the steps — as if they put the videos on slow motion, pause, and freeze, saying, 'I'm going to get that step!' They were doing the exact choreography! It blew me away."

Working so closely, the two performers became fast friends. "It was a fun project," says Paula. "Janet was a great girl to work with. The more we were around each other, she became so in tune to what I was doing that it became second nature. She was my prize student and she worked her butt off for me! The end result is that we made each other look extremely good."

They sure did! In fact, thanks to Janet's stylish videos, Paula's smooth moves caught the attention of other influential people in the music biz. Pretty soon, Paula's phone was ringing off the hook with a string of business propositions! Actually, it was her *mom's* phone that rang off the hook. Since her mother was still listed in the phone book, prospective clients called her first!

"It was such a crazy time," laughs Paula.

"I had no representation, no agent, no manager . . . so my mom would get all these phone calls, and she would call me up all frantic and all, saying, 'Paula, Paramount Pictures is on the phone — they want to know what your rates are!' So I would tell her, 'Just pretend you're my agent! Make up something!' "

Paula had more work than she had ever dreamed possible. Her involvement with a host of musicians took off, throwing her into a nonstop schedule of auditions, production meetings, rehearsals, and shootings. In fact, this young lady was so busy, she remembers having to *turn work away*! Paula had reached superstar status, and everyone wanted a part of her.

Caught up in such a whirlwind of excitement, never for a moment did Paula Abdul forget the people who helped her come this far. "It was the work with the Lakers that first opened all the doors for me," says Paula. "I'm still grateful to them and to the Jacksons for giving me those first important breaks."

Over the following few months, Paula was one of the most sought after young choreographers in the country! She created smooth moves for such celebrities as Debbie Gibson, Duran Duran, Tracey Ullman, George Michael, Aretha Franklin, ZZ Top, INXS, the Pointer Sisters, Luther Vandross, and Dolly Parton — not to mention her work with famous, hot Hollywood actors, too! Kevin Costner, Eddie Murphy, Arnold Schwarzenegger, Arsenio Hall, Dan Aykroyd, and Tom Hanks are just a few of the celebs that Paula calls her "students." "Paula," Tom Hanks once told her when the two met at a restaurant, "my biggest claim to fame is that you once choreographed me!"

What's her secret? Insight. By closing her eyes, Paula can envision the best steps to match the style of the performer she is choreographing for. "My choreography," explains Paula, "suits men very well, but the women who can do it are damn hard, strong dancers. It's extremely athletic and it combines a careful balance of femininity with an 'I can do what the guys can do' attitude. When I choreographed that style for Janet, it worked really well for her and it went with the music. I present a little bit more femininity in my choreography for myself."

"When I'm choreographing for a video," she adds, "I always have to remember that my work gets cut out a lot. You have to choreograph with that in mind and just make each second count."

4.
Straight Up . . .
and Up . . . and Up!

In 1987, Paula felt that it was time for a change. She wanted to come out from behind the scenes and try her hand at being the star. It's not that she minded choreographing for other people, it's just that during her entire life she had always dreamed of being a peformer herself. "Deep down, in the back of my mind," she said, "I knew [choreographing for others] was an avenue for me to do other things as well."

The first step, she knew, would be going into the recording studio and cutting her own album. "I loved choreography," she admits, "but I wanted to be a performer. My idols were people who could do many things — sing, dance, act, choreograph. Growing up, the people I idolized were the Judy Garlands, the Shirley MacLaines, the

Fred Astaires, the Gene Kellys. In order to be a star back in those MGM days, you had to be an all-around entertainer. You had to excel in every area to be a star. Sometimes, I feel as if I was born in the wrong era!"

Paula rounded up some other female singers and set out to cut a demo tape. The result was an amateur production of "Knocked Out," which she took over to Motown Records. The executives there thought it was "cute," but passed on it anyway.

Her next stop was over at a Warner Bros. label called Virgin Records. When the Virgin execs gave the demo a listen, they liked it, too, but wanted to hear Paula solo. She went back into the studio — this time alone — and recut the song. Within days after hearing the new version, Virgin signed this promising young beauty to their label! Little did they know then that this sweet young singer with all the right moves would end up making pop history!

Finally, with a new recording contract in hand, Paula went back into the studio for a third time, and began putting together an entire album for Virgin.

Of course, in the dog-eat-dog music business you're nothing without a snappy music video to go along with your song. With that in mind, in between recording her album and choreographing for the better part of Hollywood, she got right to work on a video for "Knocked Out." " 'Knocked Out,' " says Paula, "was the start of something I did not expect." It was the start of what would be her never-ending, totally chaotic schedule!

With her new career in full swing, Paula's days moved nonstop! "I'm a workaholic and I'm aware of that," she says matter-of-factly. "But I love doing that. I work best when I'm under pressure. I get my most creative stuff done working under the gun.

"I would choreograph *The Tracey Ullman Show* from ten A.M. to two," Paula says, remembering her wild schedule back then, "then rehearse with George Michael for his [*Faith*] tour from three to five P.M., then work with the dancers in the *Coming to America* movie from seven to ten P.M. I recorded my album from midnight to four A.M.! It was insane, but maybe the album wouldn't have turned out so well if I didn't have the pressure."

Released in June 1988, Paula's first album, *Forever Your Girl*, initially bombed! The first two singles released, "Knocked Out" and "The Way That You Love Me," never even broke into the Top 40 charts. "All I ask from people I work with is honesty," says Paula, "no matter how much it hurts. So I asked, 'Is the record a stiff or what?' And the record company said, 'Paula, it ain't happening.' "

Her video for "Knocked Out" got as far as a few stints on MTV before it slowly fizzled out. Things looked bleak.

Yet Paula was optimistic. "My mother told me never to give up my dreams," she says. "And I didn't. I still had hope for the album. I mean, I just knew it was cool — it just needed the right push."

And the right push is exactly what it got! Miraculously, almost six months later, some pop stations around the country took an interest in *another* single from *Forever Your Girl*, "Straight Up," and began playing it on the air. The snazzy song — one which Paula admits she had initially hoped to release first — began to pick up a huge following. Before she knew it . . . "Straight Up" had climbed straight up to Number One!

"When the record company called me to

tell me the single went to Number One, I was sick in bed with a really high temperature," Paula remembers. "I could hardly speak! They told me, 'You have a Number One record!' and all I had the strength to say was, 'Oh . . . great . . .!' "

Hot on the trail of that mega-successful tune, the next three singles released from that album also hit Number One: "Forever Your Girl," "Cold Hearted," and "Opposites Attract." That achievement put this deliriously happy gal into a category all her own. No other artist had ever achieved Number One status four times from one debut album! The old record of three Number One hits from a debut album was set in 1986 by Whitney Houston with *Whitney Houston*, and tied in 1989 by Milli Vanilli's *Girl You Know It's True*. Most recently, artists Mariah Carey and Wilson Phillips matched Paula's record, but with *Spellbound* cranking out the hits these days, Paula isn't worried!

5.
Tap Meets Rap

Needless to say, packed with Number One singles, the album *Forever Your Girl* made it to the Number One spot, too. In the Top Ten for 53 weeks, it was the Number One album in the country for 10 of those weeks! By then, Paula could call herself an entertainer in her own right. And while many artists would sit back and chill after such phenomenal success, there was no resting for this climbing pop star.

She went on to produce four videos to accompany her Number One songs, and even reedited and revamped her "Knocked Out" video and released it a second time! When round two of "Knocked Out" hit the MTV airwaves, it hit with a whopping TKO! Actually, all five of Paula's videos were big favorites and permanent fixtures on music video stations around the country.

Paula absolutely loved making the videos. "I get very excited about being in front of a camera," she says, "because I can be a little more daring or coy. I can be whatever I want to be."

Her video for "Straight Up" really shook up the music world when it was first released. "What was really great about 'Straight Up,'" Paula says, "is that the song had already reached the Top 20 and we hadn't even done the video yet!" Usually, an artist will make a video to help promote a newly released song. "Straight Up" was such a success on its own that the video for it was just an added extra instead of an added necessity.

One thing Paula's fabulous "Straight Up" video did for her was to introduce "Paula the Dancer" to all her fans who knew her as "Paula the Singer." It displayed her fresh talents as a hip-hop street dance technician, as well as her innovative, unique smooth style. It also started quite a few rumors about her and talk-show host Arsenio Hall, since the late-night comedian made a cameo appearance in the video! "We were just goofing around," says Paula. "Arsenio was just starting up his show at the time I was doing the video, and we were great friends so I asked him to be in it. There wasn't a script or anything; he just improvised, and we acted crazy!"

Paula will always remember making the "Forever Your Girl" video. "It was a magical video for me — I just loved working with the kids," she says. "I loved just sitting back and watching them. Sometimes, when I was having my hair and makeup done for the shoot, I would drag the stylers onto the set so I could watch the kids play while I got made up." By far her most playful video, "Forever Your Girl" shows Paula and a posse of kid dancers cuttin' up, tap-dancing, and just having a blast. "Who would have thought that a pop star would integrate tap-dancing into the mix," she boasts. "Now *that* is the coolest thing!"

"Cold Hearted," her next video to appear on the scene, shook things up even more. In it, she plays a steamy, sexy dancer auditioning for producers. The entire video rings familiar with the work of the late Bob Fosse, dancer-choreographer extraordinaire. And that was entirely Paula's intention. In fact, the "Cold Hearted" video was meant as a tribute to the great choreographer. One of Paula's greatest moments was when Bob Fosse compared her work with his early work. "Bob Fosse once made a comment about my choreography in a *People* magazine interview," Paula says. "He said that he admired my style as a young choreographer, and how I have an unpredictability in my choreography — the ability to turn right when everyone expects me to turn left. It was the biggest compliment I've ever received."

Another one of Paula's biggest thrills ever was when one of her all-time favorite idols, Gene Kelly, invited her to dinner at his home! "It was such a thrill for me," gushes the pop starlet. "I've never been so star struck in my life!" But even more exciting for Paula was when the legendary dancer called to congratulate Paula on her video "Opposites Attract." The video, which was inspired by Kelly's *Anchors Aweigh* movie where he dances with an animated mouse (Jerry, of Tom and Jerry cartoons), has Paula dancing with a very hip, funky, animated street-cat. The voice of the cat is singing rap artist M.C. Skat Kat.

"My absolute favorite dancer is Gene

Kelly," Paula says, "because he has such wonderful, beautiful grace, but he is also so athletic. I really modeled myself after him." Paula and the actor have since become very close friends, spending time together, sharing ideas, and talking about dance.

When four of her videos were completed, Paula came up with the boss idea of releasing a compilation of her videos in a home video "featurette." Adding some rare video footage of Paula kicking up her heels with the Laker Girls, a bunch of clips from backstage during the making of the videos, and some down-to-earth conversation with the starlet herself, the finished product proved to be an awesome Paula Abdul documentary! The video is called *Paula Abdul: Straight Up*, and was an instant success in the home video market, selling over a quarter of a million copies!

Paula says that one of the most frequent questions she's asked is where her video ideas come from. "I get the ideas for my videos," she explains, "by listening to the lyrical content of the songs. I can be singing and ideas come into my head and I think, 'Oh, this will be great for choreography,' and 'This would be a great video concept.'

And I collaborate with some wonderful directors who add their ideas."

Admittedly, another question Paula is usually asked is how come she looks taller in her videos than in person! "Being short," she explains, "I try to do movements in my videos that are long and angular to compensate for being five two. I've been doing that ever since I've been choreographing for myself. All the ballerinas that I looked up to growing up were these five-seven, five-eight, five-nine, and five-foot-ten-inch, lanky girls with legs up to their necks! I was always the shortest dancer. But I was this powerhouse with all this energy, and I always had to go out there and be the best I could be . . . just so people would notice me!"

It isn't hard to notice just how far Paula's innovative videos have come. In her first video for *Spellbound*, "Rush Rush," Paula continues to pay homage to the classics. This time, in her miniremake of *Rebel Without a Cause*, Paula is playing a character made famous by Natalie Wood.

"We wanted to capture some of the essence of the original film," she explained, "but make it more contemporary." For that reason, Paula hired teen heartthrob Keanu

Reeves to join her in the video, recreating the role played by James Dean. The eight-minute video ends with an epilogue in which Paula and Keanu fall in love and share a kiss.

No doubt, Paula's hottest video to date!

6.
Need a Choreographer?
Call Paula!

With the Number One album in the United States, and more TV exposure than she'd ever dreamed possible, Paula Abdul certainly didn't rest on her laurels. An admitted workaholic, this pretty lady kept on going full speed ahead, taking on project after project. By 1989 she was hailed as Hollywood's dancing Golden Girl, and one of the most admired young women in the country!

Out of all the truckloads of projects Paula was offered to choreograph, she was very selective as to which jobs she chose. One project that she quickly agreed to take on was with ace movie director Oliver Stone. The famous director had approached Paula, asking her to choreograph his movie *Evita*. "I just had a hunch about Paula," Stone said. "There is a lot of strong eighties patina on all of Paula's work, with a lot of two-step and one-step stuff that Michael Jackson started. But at the same time," he adds, "she has a solid respect for the classic musicals."

When Stone first approached Paula about working on the film, she was thrilled! *Evita* would be her very first musical! Growing up, worshipping the musical movie stars like Gene Kelly and Fred Astaire, Paula had always wished for an opportunity like this. Unfortunately, the film never got off the ground. The star actress, Meryl Streep, backed out and the movie was put on hold. "That was a six-month commitment from me. It's no longer happening because Meryl Streep backed out. She backed out due to exhaustion. Now it's postponed indefinitely. My passion was to do this," Paula says. "It meant so much to me." Meanwhile, Stone says that if the picture ever does get off the ground, Paula will be the first person he calls!

The next big project on Paula's agenda was choreographing and performing in the 1990 Academy Awards! "I was honored," she says, "and I had such a blast with it!" As with all her projects, Paula completely and wholeheartedly threw herself into the enormous task of choreographing the Oscars show. And what a smash she was that night! People joked for days about how this feisty, young dancer attracted more press and publicity that year than some of the actors and actresses nominated! Paula says it was the closest she ever came to choreographing a Hollywood musical.

In the music world, along with Madonna, Janet Jackson, Debbie Gibson, and Whitney Houston, Paula was fast becoming a dance-pop princess, helping set new dance trends across the country. Her first dance teacher, Dean Barlow, said of his prize student, "You see a new Paula video come out, and a week later the kids on *Soul Train* and *Club MTV* are doing her same steps." Barlow also says that he gets calls all the time from girls who say they want to learn the "Paula Abdul style." In fact, if she can ever find the time, Paula has expressed interest in opening her very own dance school where she could teach her funky footwork firsthand! No doubt that dance school would fill up quickly.

"Kids place a lot of importance on dance these days," Paula says. "Instead of games and sports, kids are getting into dance-offs." Paula says she gets her ideas for new steps from becoming part of what's going down in the dance club scene. "I watch kids dance," she says, "in clubs where admission is under 18, so I can see what kids are doing. Dance is no longer a spectator sport. Not wanting to sound in any way, shape, or form cocky, but I feel a part of that." And why not? It was Paula's songs and videos that have encouraged even the shyest kids to get up and get on the dance floor!

Presenting ...The Laker Girls!
(Paula is in back row center)

Paula strutting her stuff
in diet Coke commercial.

Paula is thankful for her close family ties. Here she is with her cousin and friend.

Paula mingles with Debbie Gibson at awards ceremony.

Paula with Full House star John Stamos.

7.
The Making
of *Spellbound*

After almost two years without anything
fresh from Paula, her fans were becoming
a bit restless. With the demand for Paula
Abdul so high in 1990, it was only natural
that this multitalented lady do *something*.
And something she did. Never one to disappoint her fans, Paula put together a
super-hot remix album of all her top dance
hits called *Shut Up and Dance*. That kickin'
LP sold over one million copies!

Still, Paula knew that *Shut Up and
Dance* would only satisfy her fans for a
while. It was time, she decided, to actively
begin work on a follow-up album to *Forever Your Girl* — one that would be big-
ger, better, and showcase her improved
vocal talents as well as her already

well-known dance-choreography talents.

Enter *Spellbound* — a collection of tunes from down-home funk to sweet, soulful love songs. The record, which was released at the end of May 1991, on her newly created Captive Records label, has already put this sassy songstress back at the top of the pop charts! In fact, before it was even released, her record company was so sure the LP would be a hit that they shipped one million copies out to record stores. Usually, a shipment of 100,000 means the record company knows it has a hit. By shipping a cool million, they obviously expected an explosive response!

In 1990, when she returned to the studio to begin production on *Spellbound*, Paula was nervous. So incredibly successful, *Forever Your Girl* would certainly be a tough act to follow.

She knew from the start that she wanted plenty of ballads on *Spellbound*; first and foremost because she's always wanted to sing ballads, and second, to disprove the rumors that she is just a top dance artist who can't really sing. "I'm very proud of my vocals now," Paula says. "I've worked so hard on them."

"Coming into this business," she continues, "people mostly knew about me as a successful choreographer-dancer. Moving to the front as a singer, I've been adamant about continuing to improve and grow." Of course, that goes for this dynamic lady's dancing and choreographing, too. "But the singing," she continues, "has been the most rewarding area for me. I have really built the muscle and strength in my vocals. I'm more and more confident. I take singing lessons every single day." Some days, Paula has two lessons!

Not only has Paula been taking singing lessons every day for the past two years with vocal coach Gary Catona (also actress Shirley MacLaine's vocal coach), she's even been learning to sing while jogging! This helps condition her so she can project her voice onstage while also doing some strenuous dancing!

Spellbound — the finished product — certainly proves that Miss Abdul isn't just some choreographer trying to make it as a pop singer. Sure, there were some disbelievers out there who, before *Spellbound*, weren't convinced that this gal could sing. In fact, Paula was dissed more than once by some critics. "I always, always hear, 'Paula Abdul is a mediocre singer,' " she says. But after hearing her first single released from the album, "Rush Rush," there shouldn't be any question in their minds now. "Rush Rush," aside from being a beautiful, gentle, romantic ballad, also demonstrates nicely how her vocals have matured, taking on a character all their own. "I don't profess to be this incredible singer," she says in answer to her critics, "but I think I'm a good singer and I think I'm a great performer!"

According to Paula, "Rush Rush" simply *had* to be the first single released from *Spellbound*! "People were expecting some slammin' dance tunes," she says, "which I have [on the album], too. But I was so excited when I received this song, which was written for me over a year and a half ago by The Family Stand, I wanted it first. Coming out with this ballad was the total antithesis of what people were expecting. I think the song shows so much integrity, depth, strength, and vulnerability, too.

"There was something magical that happened with it, too," she adds. "I laid down a scratch vocal for it, not intending it to be the final version, but when I sat down with it for a few days with [the producers], we decided not to touch it, because there's a raw quality to it that we didn't want to ruin."

Paula not only amazed herself while recording "Rush Rush," when she belted out some pretty hard-to-reach notes, she also startled her producers! "When I hit one of the notes in 'Rush Rush,' " says the singer, "the meter in the studio broke! The look on my face must have been something. I know my mouth was hanging open. Then I looked into the studio where my producers were, and they were laughing hysterically!

"They said, 'Bet you can't do that again!'

"And I said, 'Bet I can.' And," she says proudly, "I did!"

The producers Paula is referring to are a Brooklyn-bred funk-and-soul trio called The Family Stand. So impressed with their unique production and hip-hop musical style, Paula asked them to work on eight songs for *Spellbound*. "They had produced a couple of tracks for a new group on Virgin Records called Aftershock," Paula said. "I heard these tracks and some cuts from their own album and fell in love with them. I was blown away! I am so happy for them because they will now get their just due. They'll get credibility as both artists and producers from this."

"We were producing a group on Paula's label," says Peter Lord, who with Sandra St. Vistor and V. Jeffrey Smith make up The Family Stand. "The people there liked it a lot and they wanted us to submit songs for her. They had boxes of tapes that other writers had already sent in, but they were mostly the same old stuff she had done before. Ours were funkier, with a little more edge to them, and lyrically stronger."

The Family Stand and Paula met one night at the home of a Virgin Records executive, and Lord sat down at a piano and played a ballad for Paula called "Blowing Kisses in the Wind." She completely fell head over heels in love with the song, and immediately asked them to become part of *Spellbound*. The coming together of two such great talents was certainly a match made in heaven.

After Paula and The Family Stand finished work on "Rush Rush," Paula asked the trio to produce another song, "My Foolish Heart." She admits that she never planned to have them on practically the whole album, "but I kept on loving what they came up with," she says. "And the ballads. I'd been wanting to sing ballads all along!"

More so on *Spellbound* than on *Forever Your Girl*, Paula was in control of everything going on around her. For some artists, going into the studio can be tense and emotionally draining. But for Paula, the experience was uplifting the second time around. She explained that since there was no pressure of a deadline for *Spellbound*, things went a whole lot smoother. She had time to build up strong connections with the writers, producers, and musicians for *Spellbound* — which included such talented people as rock star Prince, Don Was, from the group Was (Not Was), r&b icon Stevie Wonder, and close friend and diet Coke commercial partner, Elton John.

"I really got to bring out the elements I wanted," Paula says of working on *Spellbound*. "The songs I wanted to sing, the lyrics I wanted to contribute, the song titles I wanted. I wanted to be more involved with this record from a creative standpoint. I wanted to grow as an artist. I wanted to have input and I wanted to write, as well."

Aside from the close relationship Paula developed during the course of working on the album with The Family Stand, she also had the amazing opportunity to work just as closely with Prince. It was the rock idol who first contacted Paula, telling her he had hoped to work with her on her new album. The two had worked together in the past, and Paula was a major fan of the Royal One. She happily agreed to let him write a song for her. "The very first song he contributed — we used," Paula says of the dance floor smash "U." "The song he delivered was just so cool, and we all really loved it."

Prince also lent his instrumental talents to "U" for *Spellbound*. The guitar you hear in the song is compliments of Prince himself! "He's really a nice guy," Paula says of her new friend. "He was fun to be with. He wanted to hear some of the other tracks and was so impressed, he kinda punched me in the arm and said, 'Sister, you singin' yer butt off on this album!' "

Overjoyed to have a fellow musician sing her praises, Paula continued working on the record with a newfound air of confidence. Even when she came up with an idea that at first everybody thought was pretty geeky, she stuck to her guns and managed to change their minds. And the result — "Will You Marry Me?" — isn't geeky at all; it's way cool. "Paula insisted that the song was the type of song all girls can relate to," said Peter Lord. "And sure enough, as soon as I mentioned it to women I knew, they loved the idea. I guess that's why she sells so many records — she's got that common touch. She knows what people want."

"When we began talking about it," Paula says about the song, "we realized there really hasn't been a song like this. It's about the girl having enough courage to ask the guy to marry her. Stevie Wonder does an incredible harmonica solo on it. I just think this will be one of those classic songs that girls are gonna request on the radio and that'll get played at people's weddings."

The offbeat, ska-flavored "Alright Tonight" is another *Spellbound* track you can count on hearing a lot, too. The song, produced by Don Was, was written especially for Paula by country and folk singer John Hiatt. The catchy tune has already been snatched up by diet Coke, for yet another excellent commercial in the Paula Abdul–Elton John collection!

"There's also a song I did with Don Was that will only be on the album outside the States, and on *For Our Children* [the album to benefit the Pediatric AIDS Foundation]," Paula explains. "It's a lullaby called 'Good Night, My Love.'"

Along with "U," the tracks from *Spellbound* that are bound to cause quite a sensation in dance clubs across the country will be the chillin' funk-with-a-message "Rock House" rap, the hip-hop title track, "Spellbound," and the electronically groovin' "Vibeology."

"I must say, I had so much fun making this album," Paula admits, "that I was in tears when it was over. It was a wonderful experience. Of course, it's over and it's just begun. . . . Now," she says, referring to her worldwide tour, "comes the hard part."

8.
On the Road!

By the time Paula's first single, "Rush Rush," hit the airwaves last May, this hard worker was already knee-deep in rehearsal for her *Spellbound* tour! "I barely had any time to worry about how the record would do," she says. The worrying she *did* do, however, really took a toll on this petite pop star's nerves. She began to experience what she calls "nervous stomach twangs." "As exciting as it is to be out there," she explains, "it's pressure. That nervous feeling in your stomach, **put**ting yourself on the line all the time."

At the start of 1991, Paula was putting herself on the line again. Beginning what would be her busiest year to date, she kicked it off by hopping a plane and jetting to Europe. "Opposites Attract" had just been released there, and Paula was en route to France to promote the single. Exhausted after just having completed *Spellbound* and leaving for France without enough rest, she came down with pneumonia and a severe ear infection and was hospitalized in Paris, and again in Milan, Italy. Paula figured out the hard way that even high-powered pop stars need a little r&r occasionally.

After recovering and returning to the States, she took some time off before strapping on her dancing shoes again. Finally well-rested, she returned to work, setting the plans in motion for her tour, which was scheduled to begin in August 1991. Luckily, Paula had already done her homework. The previous year, curious as to what her competition had been up to, she checked out both Madonna's Blonde Ambition show, and Janet Jackson's *Rhythm Nation 1814* tour. Although she was majorly impressed with both glitzy, energetic shows, Paula vowed that her own *Spellbound* tour would be the ultimate, blowing away the competition.

"It's all my dreams and efforts coming to fruition in one big event," she says of her tour. "It's going to be a visual feast, an extravaganza. I'm going to take it even further visually than people like Madonna and Janet. After I tour the States and the rest of the world, I'm going to take it to Broadway!" Her plans, she says, do include a teensy vacation for the holidays in December (this is one gal who learns from her mistakes!), but after that, it's off to Japan, Canada, Australia, and Europe.

Right now, as the *Spellbound* tour is in full swing, Paula remembers all the time and effort that went into its orchestration. Surprisingly, this is Paula's first real concert tour. That's a pretty incredible fact, since not many artists have ever had such an overwhelming debut album without going on tour to promote it. Paula, of course, was the exception to that rule! Her debut album was successful on its own merits. And while she did headline an *MTV* summer tour one year, she's never had a show she can call her own.

In putting together her stage show for the tour, her main objective was to leave her audience . . . well . . . spellbound! For this purpose, she hired Herbert Ross, former choreographer, and film director (*Steel Magnolias* and *The Turning Point*) to help her create the moves that she hopes will seize the audience's attention. "The album's title is *Spellbound*," she says. "I want people to be mesmerized!" No doubt they'll be more than mesmerized when they get a load of what this awesome entertainer has in store!

Not one to disappoint onstage, Paula has added some truly "uplifting" steps to her already thrilling stage show: acrobatics! She prepared for these exciting moves by studying aerial aerobics. Where did she come up with this unusual form of choreography? "A lot of the stuff you'll see on my tour," she says, "was envisioned while I was behind the microphone, recording the songs." In addition, Paula says she enjoyed the dazzling "flying" feats performed in concert by New Kids on the Block and Vanilla Ice, and wanted to incorporate them into her act as well. Paula executes those same, magical moves for her tour — including being hooked into a harness, like Peter Pan, for some lighter-than-air dancing! "I love being in the air," she says with a twinkle.

Paula has quite a large posse traveling with her on tour, keeping her company. Her mom, Lorraine, her sister, Wendy

Mandel, and her two nephews, Alex, five, and Austin — who is almost two — are enjoying being on tour with their famous relative and can often be found backstage. Paula says it means so much to her that they're with her during these chaotic times. But then again, Paula, her mom, and her sister have always been tight.

Paula's dad, too, keeps in touch with his daughter while she's on tour. These days, Harry Abdul lives in Big Bear, California, where he proudly follows every step of Paula's career. Paula loves to tell the story of how, when her first album came out, her dad went into a record store in Big Bear and moved all the copies of *Forever Your Girl* to the front of the racks! And with *Spellbound*, she says, he's been even more anxious. "He kept calling and saying, 'So, when's it coming out? When's it coming out?' He said he couldn't wait to hear it on the radio. You and me both, dad," she said.

Meanwhile, as Paula travels around the world, there's a brand-new Hollywood Hills home sitting empty on a hillside, waiting for its talented tenant to return from her travels. It's not a "rock house," but a peach-colored, Mediterranean-style palazzo set high in the hills, complete with a fountain, a pond stocked with rare Japanese fish, and a winding, river-like swimming pool with a swim-up bar! Her pet pug pooch, Ricky, is there, too, waiting for his beloved master to come home.

9.
The Scandal

Some say that for artists looking to make a killing at the record store, a good scandal is certainly the way to go about it. Negative publicity, they say, sells records.

Well, that may be true for some artists, but it's definitely not a notion that Paula Abdul believes in. In fact, when Paula first heard the disturbing news that Virgin Records was being sued by a disgruntled ex-backup singer of hers, she couldn't believe it.

Caught up in the biggest music scandal since the Milli Vanilli escapade, Paula was shocked, hurt, and furious at the allegations that she didn't sing on *Forever Your Girl*. "At first," says Paula, "I laughed about it because it was so ludicrous. But when I saw what was happening, it's no laughing matter."

Yvette Marine, a session singer and ex-member of Rick James' Mary Jane Girls, filed a million-dollar lawsuit against Virgin Records in April 1991, claiming that her voice was merged with Paula's on the songs "Opposites Attract," "I Need You," and "Knocked Out." Both Paula and Virgin Records firmly deny Marine's accusations. In addition, Paula thinks it's pretty malicious that this woman waited three years before coming up with her story, dropping the bombshell just three weeks before the release of *Spellbound*.

Blending two vocals together is a common studio trick done to enhance an audio track. But Virgin Records maintains that the only technology used to sweeten Paula's voice on *Forever Your Girl* was double tracking — recording the singer's voice twice to strengthen its sound.

"I sang the lead vocals on every single song on the *Forever Your Girl* album," Paula says firmly. "I put a lot of work into that album. . . . I find it particularly offensive that someone would attempt to take a shortcut to success at the expense of all the hard work that I've done.

"I think it's important for the people who voted me the 'People's Choice' award to know there's no way, in any shape or form, that I would allow myself to be discredited or let them down. But I just couldn't sit back and take it because my silence was hurting the situation. I owed it to my fans to speak out the second I heard about it."

Paula feels that her fans know her distinct-sounding voice — from hearing her sing live, and hearing her talk on talk shows and on TV — and that they couldn't possibly believe the story Marine has concocted. In fact, Virgin executives went out of their way to prove, electronically, that it is definitely Paula's voice on those songs.

Paula does admit that there are times during her live shows when she uses "augmented" vocals in addition to her own live voice. But definitely not on her album. "I'm a visual artist," she says. "I've worked with my musical director to change keys on certain songs, dropping them down so that when I'm out of breath dancing, I don't have to go for that high note. When this controversy first hit other artists, I never disputed the fact that I had some background vocals programmed into a machine. You can't sit there and expect the same vocals you hear on the album when you're singing and dancing on the stage. Every other performer in the genre does the same thing."

It's pretty obvious that her fans don't mind having to hear a line or two of Paula's voice prerecorded during the energetic extravaganza she performs onstage. If they did, they for sure wouldn't be plunking down money to see her in concert! And if they did mind . . . then how did this dynamite lady sell out this time around so darn quickly? As far as Paula is concerned, it's what her fans think that matters — not what the media thinks.

"There are things I can't control," says Paula, "such as what the media or the critics will say, but it's my responsibility to be honest and truthful and to stand up for what I believe is true. And to let my fans know I'm not going to let them down."

10.
Paying the Price
of Success

Because of the daily rapid pace of trying to juggle two careers — as a singer and as a choreographer — there's one drawback to what most people perceive as Paula's glamorous lifestyle: She has very little time left for herself, or for her family and friends.

"In the entertainment business," she explains, "your career is your relationship. I want to have the security of settling down, but it's not my time to do that right now." And dating? Well, that goes for dating, too. Although she barely has time to breathe, this attractive gal admits she'd love to find a great guy to go out with on a steady basis. But, she adds, there aren't too many great guys out there just lining up to ask her out! "I was talking with my sister," Paula said, "and she said, 'Paula, there are so many guys who would give anything to go out with you!' And I kept thinking, 'Oh, yeah? Well, where are they?' I guess they think I must already have a boyfriend or something!"

Of course, even though there's no guy in Paula's life at this time, that hasn't stopped those annoying, inevitable Hollywood romance rumors from circulating. Linked in the press to a whole brigade of famous bachelors, Paula admits that at the present moment there isn't a "significant other" in her life. But, of course, as rumors will travel, the petite singer has been romantically paired with such celebs as Arsenio Hall, Dolph Lundgren, Eddie Murphy, and John Stamos.

"Arsenio is one of my dearest friends," she says of the hip, late-night talk-show host with whom she was rumored to have been dating a few years ago, "and I hang out with him whenever there's time to hang out. We enjoy each other's company; I can talk to him about anything. He means a lot of different things to me in my life. He's the one person [who] I can tell exactly how I'm feeling, and he can understand it because he's either going through it or he's gone through it." But, as she so adamantly adds, "there is nothing romantic going on with Arsenio. He's just a very, very good friend. We've shared a lot of good times and a lot of bad times."

One relationship that *did* happen, however briefly, lasted seven months with *Full House* actor-dreamboat, John Stamos. Unfortunately, the two broke up when their careers got in the way. "We're still friends," Paula says of John. "We talk all the time." But as far as a relationship went, "Our careers just collided."

So just what does pop's leading lady look for in a leading man? "I have to find someone who has a lot of self-confidence," she says, "someone who won't be intimidated by what I represent and the money I make. Most guys meeting me think, 'What can I give her? She's got everything!' But what they can give me is the most important thing — unconditional love and support. Men expect me to be what they see in my videos. That's not me! Guys are really surprised when they find out how old-fashioned I am!"

She often thinks of finding a great guy, settling down, and having kids. "It's really hard," she says. "I feel like I'm a very accessible kind of girl. The hardest thing for any guy who tries to get involved with me is to understand the passion I have for my career. And to understand the importance of it. My work comes first, but I'm very good at working in other elements of my life, and making them equally important. I want a relationship . . . I eventually want to settle down and have two or three kids. I love kids. I really want that. But when it's right, it'll happen. I know that."

Meanwhile, Paula barely has any time to spend with the friends she *already* has! This is something this superstar feels absolutely awful about. There's Jill, her best friend from her junior high school days, and Andrea, who owns a West Hollywood clothing boutique, and Daniel, her hairdresser. Paula gave all three of these close friends a *Forever Your Girl* platinum album to thank them for their consistent love and support. And Paula was happiest when they dropped by the studio while she was recording *Spellbound* last year just to see her.

If Paula could have just one wish, it would be something along the lines of more free time for herself! What would this busy Miss do with more time on her hands? Without skipping a beat, she says, "Take dance classes! It's just a chore for me now — I don't feel comfortable just [taking classes with other people] because I feel people analyze every move I make. In order for me to take a class now, I have to take a private lesson."

Paula thanks her lucky stars that her family has agreed to join their workaholic relative on tour! If they hadn't, she would never see them. And that would simply devastate her. Especially if she couldn't see her nephews, Alex and Austin. She takes her role of Aunt Paula very seriously. Recently, she braved hordes of fans just to take Alex to see the Teenage Mutant Ninja Turtles in concert! Naturally, Paula got mobbed when she was recognized, but that didn't matter. She would do anything for her nephews. She even boasts how Alex may have inherited his aunt's dancing ability. "In his karate class," Paula says proudly, "he's the only one who can do a full split!"

Before Paula splurged on her new, luxurious, three-million-dollar-plus abode, she lived in her own apartment. "But I was working so much," she said, "I missed my family life — I was losing sight of watching my two nephews growing up." Shortly after, she left her apartment and moved in with her sister, Wendy. "I have been able to keep steady through all of this," she says of her life in the public eye, "by staying close to my family and trying to keep close to the people who loved me before I became a big star."

There was another reason Paula decided to leave her Studio City condo — she had been burglarized! In January 1989, upon returning to her apartment after an exciting night at the American Music Awards, Paula discovered that someone had broken in.

"I was heading straight for the phone machine," she remembers, "but when I flipped on the lights, it was gone." So were her jewelry, stereo, makeup, platinum albums, and several of her awards! She says that by the time her mom came to pick her up, the crime had already made the TV news. "I was even more upset by that," she said. "It struck me as terribly weird that it was important for everyone to know. For the first time, I felt really scared."

Unfortunately, success has a way of intruding on just about every aspect of a performer's personal life. Sometimes, Paula resents the intrusion. "I may not look great one day, you know, I may not want to put on my makeup or dress nice," she says. "People get all bent out of shape. They think that I can't have a bad day or be depressed like everybody else."

One thing Paula usually doesn't mind, though, is when she's recognized. She has come to understand the demands of fame. "Whenever you leave the house," she explains, "you have to accept the fact that someone is going to see or recognize you.

"You see people in your peripheral vision," she continues, "and they're watching everything you do!" She laughs, recalling a time when she was eating at a restaurant and a piece of lettuce fell out of her mouth. After trying, unsuccessfully, to push the lettuce back into her mouth, she noticed people were watching her! But this good-natured girl just thought the whole thing was so funny and started laughing. Of course, that caused the other people to laugh, too. "You really have to focus in on the person you're having lunch with," she says, "and not be concerned that there's food dripping out of your mouth!"

Once, she even went as far as to disguise herself! But she blames her signature beauty mark for always giving her away.

"I've gone to Disneyland in a pair of sunglasses, with all my hair pulled back under a hat," she laughs, "and I still hear people say, 'It's her! Look, there it is — the mole!'"

But Paula knows that the people who follow her, gawk at her, or ask for autographs are her biggest fans. "I get really touched," she says, "when the young people come up to me and say, 'I'm in dance class now, and I'm learning how to tap-dance.' And I see some senior citizens that say, 'Oh, you're that song-and-dance girl,' and they put up the okay sign. Things like that mean so much to me."

These days, Paula receives over 5,000 pieces of fan mail each week! Not to mention the countless marriage proposals, requests to sing at kids' parties, and kids begging the superstar to come to their schools. But definitely the weirdest thing, she says, was when she got a letter from a farmer who told her that he serenades his cows with her music!

"I love what I do," Paula says. "I love every aspect of it. But the most gratifying thing is to do what you want to do and get back that fan appreciation. Knowing that you're giving to the people and receiving in return. With any success, you have to weather the storm and take the hard knocks, too. That's the high price of fame and success — dealing with that.

"Everyone goes through ups and downs," she adds. "There are times when I feel that I just want to give up. The thing to realize is that [success] can happen if you stay focused and close to your heart and what you believe in.

"This business hardens a lot of people. But I love what I do and I wouldn't trade it for anything!"

11.
Forever
a Generous Girl!

Unbelievably, with barely a second to herself, Paula still finds the time to aid many charitable organizations. A very generous girl by nature, helping others is something she feels very strongly about. While she has helped dozens of charities in the past, these days she is an active participant in two causes: Little Green, and the Pediatric AIDS Foundation.

"Recently, I've become involved as spokesperson for a program called Little Green, aimed at involving young people in saving our environment. Our goals are to teach people about what's happening in their world, and to help them do things that will really make a difference. We kicked off our program in January 1991, with a 'Little

Green Is Big Time' writing and arts competition, and we will be doing other things to raise awareness of the environment in the coming months."

Paula became more aware of the problems facing our environment when she was filming her "Forever Your Girl" video in 1989. "I worked closely with kids on that video, teaching them to dance, and it really made me wonder about their future. What kind of world are we going to leave them? We need to do what we can right now to clean up the environment and make the world a more beautiful, safer place to live."

Paula hopes more kids will join her in her efforts to clean up the environment. She came up with the smart idea of including a punch-out postcard on all her *Spellbound* albums and CD packaging that can be sent to Little Green for more information about joining the organization.

If you would like to know more about joining Little Green, write to: Sebastian's Little Green, Department LG, 6109 DeSoto Avenue, Woodland Hills, CA 91367.

When she's not worrying about keeping the planet clean, Paula tends to matters equally important. She is majorly concerned about a terrible disease that is affecting million of people in the world — many of them children.

Back in 1987, Paula met a very special little girl. Her name was Ariel Glaser, and she died in 1990 — at age seven — from AIDS. Since then, Paula has become a member of the Pediatric AIDS Foundation, which helps children who have AIDS fight the disease. In May 1991, Paula got together with a bunch of famous singers to record an album called *For Our Children*. All the money made from *For Our Children* will go to the Pediatric AIDS Foundation.

Paula's contribution to the record is a beautiful lullaby called "Good Night, My Love." Rocker Don Was produced the song for Paula. Both singers are equally proud to be a part of such a special project.

"A few years ago," Paula says, "I had the opportunity to meet Ariel Glaser on the set of the film *Running Man*. She'd come down as often as she could to visit her father, [actor-director] Paul Michael Glaser, and she had a real fascination with the dancers I was working with.

"When I found out she had AIDS, I was stricken, and I promised myself I'd do everything possible to help other young people afflicted with that terrible disease. I wanted to get involved to the best of my ability and to let them know that my heart is with them. I'm gratified that the Pediatric AIDS Foundation has grown through the efforts of Elizabeth Glaser (Ariel's mom) and many others who have given their heartfelt energies to this important cause. I'm proud to be a part of it."

If you would like to learn more about the Pediatric AIDS Foundation, Paula urges you to write: Pediatric AIDS Foundation, 2407 Wilshire Boulevard, Suite 613, Santa Monica, CA 90403.

12.
Hollywood-bound

A chart-busting new album, a block-busting, brand-new tour — where does Paula go from here? How can she top her latest, skyrocketing achievements? Good question. Naturally, for this talented, al-ways rising star, her next step is . . . Hol-lywood! Is the world ready for Paula Abdul on the big screen? You bet!

"I want to start small," she says, ever so cautiously. "I'm not looking to jump into the movies and make mine a short career. I really want it to last."

With a schedule that is literally booked solid for the next two years, it's a wonder this superstar can find room for any movie projects, but she has! Aside from devoting herself to her current tour and its antici-pated smash finale on Broadway, and creating brand-new videos for *Spellbound*, she has also managed to fit acting lessons into her appointment-jammed days. There are quite a few movie projects in the works for this top-notch entertainer, and she wants to be ready!

"I've got development projects with both Universal and Disney for my film debut," this attractive singer reveals. "But my first movie role will have nothing to do with song and dance. I think that's very important. Then I can establish myself as an actress. But after the first couple of nonmusical films . . . I'm going to do a full-blown musical!"

Maybe that's why Paula has been talking with friend and mentor Gene Kelly about possible acting projects. If anyone knows musicals, it's the legendary Broadway and film star. She's also working with director and good friend James Brooks (*Broadcast News* and *Terms of Endearment*) on a different movie project.

"I don't want to play myself," she says of her ideal debut role. "For my first project, I want to co-star. I want a good support system. I want to be surrounded by a great cast and a great director. I want to work in an ensemble — I don't want all the weight to be on my shoulders."

Meanwhile, Paula is simply swamped with offers to do a *Paula Abdul Story* — but she doesn't see that happening just yet. "I don't want a film that's going to star Paula Abdul," she says. "I want it to be the kind of thing where people will look and say, 'Oh, my God, that's Paula Abdul in that film!'"

Universal Pictures is developing a feature film for her, too — but this is one flick that the petite starlet definitely wants in on. This film would reunite the dancer with her animated video partner, M.C. Skat Kat from her video "Opposites Attract." Admittedly, this is one project Paula is very excited to begin.

Last summer, however, Paula spent some time trying to work out a project that doesn't involve movies or records or videos at all. This dancing doll, who sometimes dreams dance sequences in her sleep, has hopes of opening a dance school and foundation in Los Angeles. Her plan is to create a place where both kids and adults can come to study the performing arts. Paula and her sister plan to teach a few of the "master" dance classes there themselves! And stepping along those lines, Paula would like to introduce her very own line of dance and gym shoes, too.

In addition, Paula has publicly expressed interest in doing a televison project. But until this working woman has a few months to spare, the only way you'll see her strut her stuff on the small screen is if you happen to catch her latest diet Coke commercial! Back in 1990, this gorgeous girl signed up her sweet smile and bubbling persona to endorse such well-known products as diet Coke and L.A. Gear. She appeared in her first diet Coke TV commercial with rocker Elton John, and she has assured us that there are more soda-pop projects to come starring this pop duo!

Success has been very good to Paula Abdul, and she has handled her bout with stardom beautifully and commendably. Those who know her now and knew her when, agree that this is one celeb who has not changed her demeanor in any way. Indeed, part of Paula's charisma is due to her down-to-earth honesty — even in a business where others tend not to be so honest. "I wasn't cut out for this business," she says. "I always wanted to be a dancer, but being short and not being a starlet-type-looking girl, I knew it would be harder for me —

that I would have to be really good at something to make people notice me.

"I never knew I would achieve all of this, this way," she adds. "I never thought I'd get to a point where I was fulfilling all my dreams. It's been great. It's been overwhelming."

And now, on the verge of jumping back into the spotlight once again as her tour travels around the globe to be met by critics everywhere, this tiny dynamo can only wonder: "How in the heck did I do it last time?"

But she knows. "It just fell together last time," she remembers with a smile. "I'll take things day by day. And everything will fall together again."

Of course it will, Paula.

Paula Abdul:
Up Close and Personal

Full Name: Paula Julie Abdul
Birthdate: June 19, 1963
Astrological Sign: Gemini
Birthplace: Los Angeles, California
Height: 5'2"
Weight: 105 lbs
Hair: Naturally brown
Eyes: Brown
Marital Status: Single
Family: Parents, Harry and Lorraine; Sister, Wendy; Nephews, Alex and Austin
Nationality: Combination of Brazilian and Syrian (on her dad's side); Jewish and French Canadian (on her mom's side). "I'm a mutt," she giggles.
Favorite Food: Chinese
Favorite Musician: Michael Jackson
Favorite Movie: *Big*

Her Daily Schedule: Starts her day with an exercise class or dance lesson, an acting lesson, and a vocal lesson. Afternoons are usually filled up with meetings, film producers or directors. While touring, there are also rehearsals, sound checks, and lots of traveling.

She Hates: "When people lie or misinterpret my shyness for aloofness. What irritates me most is that just because I'm in the public eye doesn't mean I can't have a bad day like everyone else."

Not Many People Know: That famous singer Michael Bolton (who is currently making his way up the pop charts, too) used to baby-sit for Paula!

Free Time: "With the little free time I have, I usually go to the movies, or bike riding by the beach." Paula also loves to spend time with her nephews.

What Gets Her Down: "When I realize I miss a lot of my friends and I don't get a chance to hang out with them, or when I feel I want to focus on a relationship."

Inspirations: In the music industry: Stevie Wonder, Carole King, the Jacksons, and Aretha Franklin. In the dance world: Gene Kelly, Fred Astaire, Cyd Charisse, Liza Minnelli, Leslie Caron, and Shirley MacLaine.

On Her Pop Crossover Status: "I feel fortunate that I'm embraced by everyone, that everyone can identify with me — on a dance level, on a creative level, having a multifaceted career, a multiethnic background, too. Kids of all backgrounds say, 'You inspire me.' And that makes me feel great."

Hanging Out Clothes: Jeans, shirts, and boots.

What She Looks for in a Guy: "I have to find someone who has a lot of self-confidence — someone who won't be intimidated by what I represent and the money I make."

Most Gratifying Career Aspect: " . . . has been doing exactly what I want to do and getting positive feedback from the audience. The most honest reactions I get come from my fans, and that's what helps me see the big picture of where I want to go with my career."

Awards, Accolades, Accomplishments

1991 Grammy Award, National Academy of Recording Arts and Sciences: Best Music Video for "Opposites Attract"

1991 People's Choice Award: Favorite Female Musical Performer

1990 American Music Award: Favorite Pop Rock Artist; Favorite Dance Artist

1990 National Academy of Motion Picture Arts and Sciences: Choreography

1990 Emmy Award: Outstanding Choreography for The American Music Awards

1989 Emmy Award: Outstanding Choreography for *The Tracey Ullman Show*

1989 MTV Awards: Best Female Artist;

Best Dance Video; Best Choreographer; Best Editing

1989 National Academy of Dance: Choreographer of the Year

Miscellaneous Achievements:

Billboard **Music Video Award:** Best Female Video; New Artist Video; Choreography; Editing

Rolling Stone **Reader's Poll:** Best Female Singer; Best New Female Singer; Best-Dressed Female Rock Artist; Sexiest Female Artist

Soul Train **Award**

Billboard **Chart #1 Single:** "Straight Up"; "Forever Your Girl"; "Cold Hearted"; "Opposites Attract"

Billboard **Chart Single:** "The Way That You Love Me"

Billboard **Chart Single:** "Knocked Out"

"Straight Up" went platinum.

"Forever Your Girl"; "The Way That You Love Me"; "Cold Hearted"; and "Opposites Attract" went gold.

Choreography
Highlights

Films:
The Doors (1991)
She's Out of Control (1989)
The Karate Kid Part III (1989)
Coming to America (1988)
Big (1988)
Bull Durham (1988)
The Running Man (1987)

TV:
The Academy Awards Show (1990)
The Tracey Ullman Show (1987–1989)

Videos:
"Straight Up" (1989)
"Forever Your Girl" (1989)
"Cold Hearted" (1989)
"The Way That You Love Me" (1989)
"Knocked Out" (1989)

"Opposites Attract" (1989)

"Roll With It" for Steve Winwood (1988)

"Velcro Fly" for ZZ Top (1986)

"Nasty"; "When I Think of You"; "Control"; and "What Have You Done For Me Lately" for Janet Jackson (1986)

Discography

Forever Your Girl (1988):
"Straight Up"
"Forever Your Girl"
"The Way That You Love Me"
"Cold Hearted"
"Opposites Attract"
"Knocked Out"
"I Need You"
"State of Attraction"
"Next to You"
"One or the Other"

Shut Up and Dance (1990):
"Cold Hearted" (Quiverin' 12″)
"Straight Up" (Ultimix Mix)
"One or the Other" (1990 Mix)
"Forever Your Girl" (Frankie Foncett)
"Knocked Out" (Pettibone 12″)

"The Way That You Love Me" (Houseafire Edit)
"Opposites Attract" (1990 Mix)
1990 Medley Mix

Spellbound (1991):
"Rush Rush"
"U"
"Will You Marry Me?"
"Blowing Kisses in the Wind"
"Alright Tonight"
"Rock House"
"The Promise of a New Day"
"Vibeology"
"My Foolish Heart"
"To You"
"Spellbound"

"Good Night, My Love" — a lullaby recorded for Walt Disney Records *For Our Children* album, a benefit for the Pediatric AIDS Foundation.

Videography

"Knocked Out"
"Straight Up"
"Forever Your Girl"
"Cold Hearted"
"Opposites Attract"
"Rush Rush"

Paula Abdul: Straight Up — featuring a compilation of four videos: "Knocked Out," "Straight Up," "Forever Your Girl," "Cold Hearted."

If you would like to find out more about Paula Abdul, write to:

The Paula Abdul Fan Club
14755 Ventura Boulevard, #1–710
Sherman Oaks, CA 91403